For the happy little cubs of Québec,
Anabelle and Nicolas
— C. J.

For Ariel Fruit
— M.B.

Originally published in France as *Ourson Le Terrible* copyright © 2016 by Kaléidoscope.
Text and illustrations by Christian Jolibois and Marianne Barcilon.
First published in English in 2017 by Peter Pauper Press, Inc.

Published by Peter Pauper Press, Inc.
202 Mamaroneck Avenue
White Plains, New York 10601
U.S.A.

Published in the United Kingdom and Europe by Peter Pauper Press, Inc.
c/o White Pebble International
Unit 2, Plot 11 Terminus Rd.
Chichester, West Sussex PO19 8TX, UK

Library of Congress Cataloging-in-Publication Data Available

ISBN 978-1-4413-2318-7
Manufactured for Peter Pauper Press, Inc.
Printed in Hong Kong

7 6 5 4 3 2 1

Visit us at www.peterpauper.com

TEDDY THE TERRIBLE

CHRISTIAN JOLIBOIS • MARIANNE BARCILON

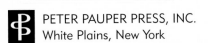 PETER PAUPER PRESS, INC.
White Plains, New York

Do you hear all that noise?
All that shouting and clatter?
Forest creatures are frightened.
What could be the matter?

"The monster is coming!" They yell and they shout.
"The monster is coming! Save yourself and get out!"

What could it be that frightens them so?
That's got them all shivering from their heads to their toes?
A sneaky hunter tracking this bunch?
A big hungry ogre looking for lunch?

No, no, my friends, it's much worse than that.
It's not a hunter, an ogre—or even a rat!

It's not very big,
about three feet tall,
but it's the meanest and grouchiest
bully of all!

He's fearsome, ferocious,
and not at all nice.
He's downright atrocious.
Don't look his way twice.

He'll constantly pick on you
for no rhyme or reason.
Whatever the day,
whatever the season.

Here he comes now,
with a roar and a growl.
It's Teddy the Terrible,
out on the prowl!

"Hey, what are YOU lookin' at?"

"Well, hello little froggies,"
Teddy says with a smile.
"You've been sunning out here
for a very long while."

"I think it's time you all take a dip.
One, two, three—try not to slip!"

Then Teddy starts a serious quake,
with a shove, and a push, and three fearsome shakes!

"Looks like a storm is coming to town.
It's raining squirrels—
everyone come on down!"

"Now, c'mon little fishy,
I've got a plan.
Let's hold your breath,
for as long as you can."

But what he said next,
was the absolute worst.
Even for Teddy,
this was a first.

"Your mother has left you.
She packed up her sack.
She flew far away.
She's NOT coming back."

Mid-day had arrived—it was time to find lunch.
"Ah-ha!" Teddy cried. "I smell mushrooms to munch."

"Beat it and scram!"
he told the young boars.
"These mushrooms are mine!
All mine, and not yours!"

GROARRR!

When he was done,
and filled to the brim,
he stomped on the rest
with a chuckle and grin.

"Now no one at all
will be able to eat.
I've crushed each 'shroom
with my two mighty feet."

Teddy the terror
continued his day,
picking on everyone
who got in his way.

The poor little pheasant
lost his best feather.
"Pluck! Pluck!" went Teddy.
"Now my teeth are much better."

Confused and alarmed,
by Teddy's loud shout,
the moles didn't know
WHAT he was screaming about.

But when nighttime fell
each animal went home.
All except Teddy
who lived all alone.

Early next morning,
the bully was back.
"Ha! Ha!" Teddy said,
"It's time to attack!"

"This pile of ants,
could use a swift kick.
It would even be better,
if I had a big stick!"

"Uh-oh," Teddy gulped.
"Now what have I done?"
He froze in his tracks,
with nowhere to run.

"Who woke me up?"
growled the big bear.
"Who dares disturb me?"
she asked with a stare.

"This is no way
to treat one another.
You've been very rude.
Now, where is your MOTHER?"

"I'm just an orphan.
You put me down, Miss!
I don't need anyone,
I'm Teddy. The Fearless!"

"Oh, so you are the Terror,
I keep hearing about,
picking on others,
being naughty, no doubt.

Listen young Teddy,
that's enough now—no more.
It's time you were given,
what you needed before."

"You leave me alone,
and let me down, Miss!"

But before Teddy knew it,
she gave him a . . .

Teddy's knees wobbled
as he stumbled about.
He felt warm and fuzzy,
both inside and out.

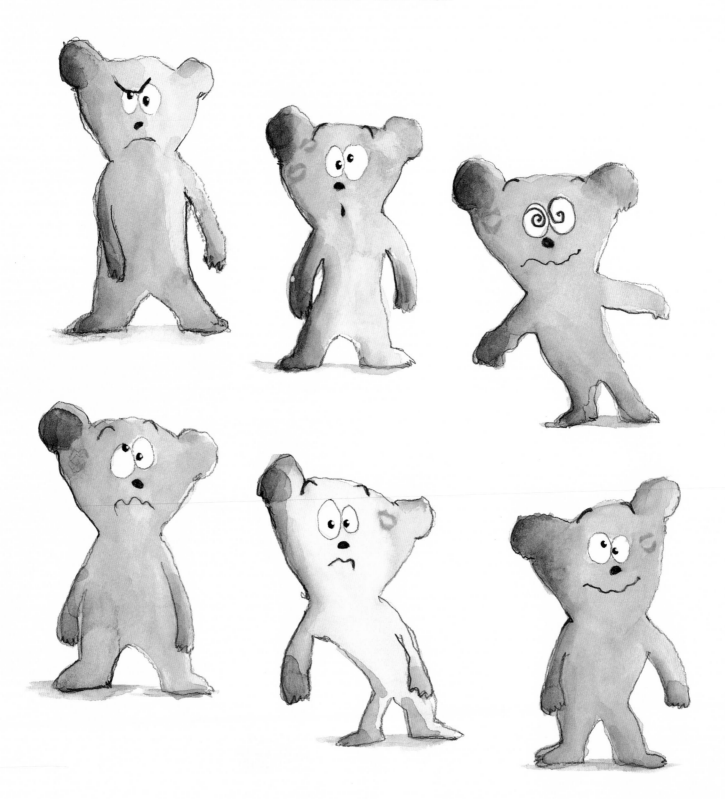

"What was THAT?"
he asked in a daze.
Teddy was floating,
up, down, and sideways.

"Given with love,
it will make you feel bliss.
It's commonly called
a smooch, peck, or kiss.

And a kiss can be given
without rhyme or reason,
whatever the day,
whatever the season."

Teddy had never
felt this good before.
But one thing was certain,
he wanted lots more!

So kind mama bear
counted kisses to ten.
Teddy smiled and said . . .

"Again,
please.
Again!"

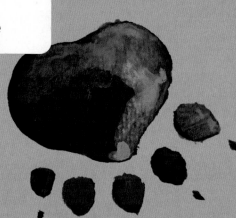